This Igloo book belongs to:

....

igloobooks
.com

Published in 2012
by Igloo Books Ltd
Cottage Farm
Sywell
NN6 0BJ
www.igloo-books.com

SHE001 0812
10 9 8 7 6 5 4 3 2 1
ISBN 978-0-85780-548-5

Printed and manufactured in China

Illustrated by Helen Poole
Written by Elizabeth Dale

Bedtime Stories for Girls

igloobooks.com

Contents

Penny's Perfect Pony ... Page 6

Princess Lucy's Cupcake Crisis ... Page 14

Amanda's Amazing Glasses.... Page 22

Bella the Bridesmaid ... Page 30

Dancing Della ... Page 38

The Purrfect Playmate ... Page 46

The King's Birthday Cake ... Page 54

Tilly's Magic Tiara ... Page 62

The Enchanted Wishing Bed ... Page 70

Sammy the Star ... Page 78

Fairy Cakes ... Page 84

Summer and Starlight ... Page 92

Message in a Bottle ... Page 100

Suzy's Special Stone ... Page 108

What's Wrong, Waggy-Tail? ... Page 116

Megan's Magic Bracelet ... Page 124

The Mermaidettes ... Page 132

Beautiful Ballerinas ... Page 138

Lisa's Surprising Spells ... Page 146

Princess Posy and the Undoing Potion ... Page 152

Penny's Perfect Pony

Penny wished her rocking horse was a real pony. She had always wanted one, but her parents said it was too expensive. Penny rocked on the toy horse, pretending she was in a pony jumping competition. She leapt over the jumps and sped to the finish, winning the first prize rosette. Penny sighed, patting the wooden horse's head. "I wish you were real," she said, sadly, stroking his mane.

Just then, the rocking horse started to glitter and sparkle. Penny gasped as the pony began to toss his head and whinny. Suddenly, he had become a real pony.

Penny held tightly onto the pony's reins as he trotted towards the window, leaping out into the sky. As they soared over the town, Penny wondered if they would go to Fairy Land.

Penny's Perfect Pony

As they flew into the distance, Penny could make out amazing princess castles, sparkling lakes and brightly colored fields. Cute dragons fluttered in the sky and as Penny looked down, some teddies waved at her. They were having a picnic of delicious cakes. Beside them was a beautiful unicorn with a sparkly horn. He looked up at Penny and whinnied.

Just then, Penny noticed some fairies flying towards her. "Welcome to Fairy Land!" they called to Penny, smiling.

"I'm Crystal," said one of the fairies, smiling at Penny. "I'm going to show you all of Fairy Land." For the rest of the day, Penny paddled in glittering lakes made of lemonade, tasted chocolate fountains and played with the little dragons, who loved to dance. Penny had so much fun that when Crystal began to lead them back, she was upset. "Don't worry," whispered Crystal. "We have a special surprise for you."

When they arrived at the fairy's home, Penny could see some horse jumps and a proper race course.

"We're having a pony competition," cried Crystal, showing Penny her own unicorn. Penny was so excited. She'd always wanted to take part in a pony race and now she even had her own pony to ride. Even though Penny had never jumped before she soon got the hang of it, flying over the jumps perfectly.

After the race, Crystal led Penny into a beautiful tent. It was decorated with ribbons and there were lots of cakes and treats. The fairies were dancing and smiling with one of the dragons from earlier. Crystal took Penny to the middle of the room and gave her a beautiful rosette.

She had won the pony competition! "Thank you so much," said Penny, smiling happily at Crystal.

Just then, Penny felt sleepy. She yawned and closed her eyes. When she opened them, she was back in her bedroom. She gazed sleepily across the room at the rocking horse and thought about all of the wonderful things she had seen and done that night. Crystal said she could go back to Fairy Land whenever she wanted and Penny couldn't wait for her next adventure.

Penny snuggled up in bed, imagining she was flying over the beautiful valleys of Fairy Land. As she began to drift off to sleep, her hand clasped around the rosette she had won in the pony competition. "I bet no one will believe how good I am at show jumping," she thought, smiling to herself as she fell into a deep sleep. She was the luckiest girl in the world.

Princess Lucy's Cupcake Crisis

It was the day of the Annual Rose Ball and everyone in the palace was busy. Princess Lucy couldn't wait for the ball, but it was hours away and she was bored of everyone rushing around. No-one would play with her. Lucy tried to speak to her mother as she hurried past with rollers in her hair. "I can't talk now," said the queen. "My hair is a disaster."

Lucy tried not to giggle as she decided to look for the king. She found him in the corner of the ballroom, giving orders to the decorators. "Hello, Lucy," he said, as she wandered over. "I'm so busy. I need to decorate the hall and fit my suit at the same time!" The king shrugged his shoulders as he walked away, followed by a group of tailors hastily trying to fix his jacket.

Lucy sighed. Maybe her sisters would have time to play with her?

Princess Lucy's Cupcake Crisis

Lucy found May and Angela getting ready for the ball in the queen's bedroom. "Can I get ready with you?" Lucy asked her sisters. The girls nodded, paying more attention to the mirror than Lucy.

Lucy started to put on the queen's clothes and soon she was wearing all of her beautiful rings. She twirled around the room, laughing and smiling. When she had finished, Lucy was bored again and May and Angela were still applying make-up.

Just then, Lucy smelled something wonderful. She followed the smell to the kitchen, finding Cook baking delicious cakes for the Rose Ball. Lucy ran over to help her scoop the yummy mixture into the cases. Cook and Lucy laughed and joked as they worked together and finally the cakes were ready to put in the oven.

"Yum," said Lucy, tasting a cupcake. Suddenly, she looked down at her finger. Her mother's ring was missing!

17

"Oh, no!" cried Lucy. The ring must have dropped into the cake mixture. She looked in horror at the mountain of cupcakes that Cook had decorated, ready for the ball. She would have to eat all of them to find the ring. Lucy took a deep breath and bit into a cupcake, but the ring wasn't there. She picked up another and another, but she couldn't find the queen's ring anywhere.

Soon, Lucy was feeling a little sick. She had eaten loads
of the cupcakes, but she still couldn't find her mother's
ring anywhere. Lucy didn't know what to do. She was just about
to cry when the queen walked into the room. "What's wrong,"
she asked Lucy, giving her a big cuddle. Lucy looked at her
mother and decided to tell her everything.
"Don't worry," said the queen, laughing. "I have an idea."
She took Lucy's hand and led her into the busy ball room.

In the ballroom, all of the guests looked splendid. They laughed and giggled in the hall as they waited for the queen.
All around the room, tables were piled high with dainty, little cupcakes. Not that Lucy wanted to eat any more cakes!

Suddenly, the queen clapped her hands. "Welcome," she said, as the guests turned towards her. Lucy gulped, feeling nervous as she wondered what her mother was about to say.

"We are going to play a game," said the queen, smiling. "One of these delicious cupcakes has a special ring, hidden inside of it. Whoever finds the ring, can keep it for themselves." Everyone happily tucked into the delicious cupcakes, even Lucy.

Suddenly, there was shout. "I've found the ring!" Lucy cried. The queen smiled, "It's yours now," she said to Lucy. "You have been very honest today and I am very proud of you."

Amanda's Amazing Glasses

Amanda was excited as she sat in the optician's chair. She had always wanted glasses and now she was finally getting her eyes tested. Cassie, a girl in her class, had an amazing sparkly, pink pair and Amanda couldn't wait to get some of her own.

My Jones, the optician, put a strange pair of glasses on her eyes and held up a big white board with lots of letters, telling her to read them out. Amanda gasped. For once, she could actually read the letters!

Next, Mr Jones flicked a switch on the glasses and held up a board with farmyard animals. Amanda could see it even better than before. Finally, Mr. Jones peered right into her eyes. "Well, Amanda!" he said. "You do need glasses." Amanda smiled and jumped out of the chair. "Hooray," she cried, smiling.

Amanda's Amazing Glasses

Mr Jones lead Amanda to a stand and showed her all of the pretty glasses. None of them were as cool as Cassie's.
Just then, Amanda saw a sparkly pair with little hearts in the corners. There was even a pink case with fairies on it! She tried the glasses on, looking in the mirror. "These look absolutely perfect," said Amanda, smiling. "They must be very special to have fairies and hearts on them," she thought happily.

Amanda's Amazing Glasses

Amanda loved her new glasses. She was amazed by how clearly she could see. She rushed into the garden, looking everywhere. She could see all the beautiful flowers, but there was something else in the garden, too. As Amanda looked closely, she could see something fluttering. Suddenly, she realized there were lots of dainty fairies, flying all around her. One of the fairies fluttered over to Amanda. "Hello," said the fairy to Amanda.

"I'm Twinkle," said the fairy. "Would you like to play?"
She beckoned to Amanda to follow her to the bottom of
the garden. They came to a big tree with a picnic blanket laid
out in front of it. There were lots of fairies flying everywhere.
Twinkle fluttered into the tree, opening the window and
waving at Amanda.

Amanda was so excited. She sat down and told the fairies all
about her glasses. "I could never see you before," she explained.

"Well, now you can," giggled Twinkle. "Would you like to learn how to fly?" she asked Amanda.

"Yes, please," Amanda cried, smiling excitedly.

Twinkle fluttered into the air and told Amanda to close her eyes tightly. "Imagine you're flying!" Twinkle cried.

When Amanda opened her eyes, she was in the air. Twinkle was beside her, giggling as they floated through the blue sky.

Amanda was tingling with excitement as she soared past fluffy, white clouds. Just then, Twinkle pointed downwards and they fluttered to the ground together, landing in the middle of a forest clearing. As Amanda looked around, she could see more and more fairies. The clearing was decorated with amazing ribbons and there were lots of delicious looking cakes and treats everywhere. Amanda smiled, running across the grass towards a cool looking apple tree that had purple leaves.

Amanda's Amazing Glasses

"We're having a banquet," Twinkle said, smiling at Amanda and introducing her to all of her fairy friends.

Amanda couldn't believe how lucky she was. As she danced with Twinkle and the fairies, Amanda thought about her glasses with the hearts and fairy case. She had known that they were special glasses, but she was so excited to find out that they were magic, too! "I love my amazing glasses," she thought, smiling and laughing with her new fairy friends.

Bella the Bridesmaid

Bella sighed, "I'd love to be a bridesmaid," she said, as she arranged flowers in the local church. Bella's mother was a wedding planner and Bella loved to help her get everything ready.

The church looked so beautiful that Bella couldn't help daydreaming. She imagined that she was a beautiful bridesmaid with an amazing dress. In her dreams, she wasn't an ordinary girl, she was as beautiful as a princess. Bella looked at the flowers she was arranging and imagined they were her very own bouquet.

All of these times Bella had helped her mother decorate the church and all of the times she had watched the beautiful bridemaids walk down the isle. She wanted to be a bridesmaid so much!

Suddenly, Bella and her mother heard a noise. Clip-clop!
"It's a horse-drawn carriage," whispered Bella, as the carriage
appeared around the corner. It was drawn by an adorable white
horse and was decorated with beautiful flowers and pretty
pink ribbons. Sitting inside, the bride looked like princess in
her amazing pink, shimmery dress and sparkly tiara.
Bella watched her sparkle as she walked towards the church.

As the bride got closer, Bella could hear what she was saying. "Whoever heard of a bride without a bridesmaid?" she cried. "What are we going to do with this beautiful dress?" Bella gasped as she saw the dress. It had sequins sparkling all over the long, silky skirt. It was just like the dress in her dream. Suddenly, the bride turned around and looked straight at Bella.

"Hello," said the bride, smiling at Bella. "I'm Laura," she said.
"I was wondering if you would like to be my bridesmaid?" Bella
nodded, she could hardly speak she was so excited.
She grabbed the dress and hurried into an empty room.
The beautiful bridesmaid dress shimmered and sparkled, the
sequins twinkled like tiny diamonds and it fitted perfectly.
Bella twirled and spun in the mirror, admiring her reflection.
She looked like a beautiful fairytale princess.

Bella had never felt so proud as she walked down the aisle behind Laura. Bella loved the little hearts on her tiara and her bouquet was beautiful. It was just like her daydreams, she thought, smiling brightly.

At the end of the service, Bella walked back down the aisle with the bride. She was sure she could hear someone sobbing quiet tears of joy. As she turned around, she could see her mother smiling happily.

When it was time for the photos, Laura wanted Bella in all of them. After they had taken all of the serious photos, there were some of just Bella and Laura. They threw their bouquets in the air and laughed. Then, just as Bella thought it was time to go home, Laura called to Bella's mother. "Come on, mother of the bridesmaid," said Laura, grabbing Bella's mother's hand and pushing her in front of the camera.

Finally, all of the wedding photos were finished. As Bella left, Laura gave her a cuddle. "Thank you for being the best bridesmaid," she said. "Please keep the dress and the photos to remember today."

How could Bella ever possibly forget, when today had been the best day of her life? She couldn't wait to show her friends all of the amazing photos of Bella, the beautiful bridesmaid!

Dancing Della

One day, Della was walking past the shoe shop in her village, when suddenly she stopped. In the window was a lovely, brand new pair of purple tap shoes. "Wow, I'd love those shoes," thought Della, smiling. Just then, she saw her friend, Lisa across the road. "Hi, Lisa!" Della cried, waving. "Come and look at these gorgeous shoes." Lisa just shook her head. "No, thanks," she said.

Della noticed that Lisa looked really unhappy. "What's the matter?" she asked.

"I don't know," replied Lisa, "I just feel really fed up. It must be the weather." With that, Lisa walked off down the high street.

"Oh well," said Della. "I'll go and look at the shoes. I've been saving my pocket money for ages and I'm sure I'll have enough money to buy them." Della went back across the road and opened the door of the little shop.

Dancing Della

"Please can I try on the purple tap shoes in the window?" asked Della, smiling at the assistant.

"Yes, of course," the assistant replied, taking the shoes from the window display.

Della smiled as she slipped on the purple shoes. They fitted her perfectly. Suddenly, Della felt a tingling in her feet and before she knew it she was dancing around the shop.

Della giggled, paying for the shoes as she tapped and whirled.

Dancing Della

Della loved the shoes so much she decided to wear them home. Even outside, on such a grey day, they sparkled. With every step she took there was a lovely click, the shoes seemed to tap out a beautiful rhythm as she walked. She skipped onto the crossing, her shoes perfectly tapping out every move she made.

Della smiled. She was so happy with her brand new shoes that she didn't notice that people were starting to stare at her.

Della danced faster and faster and her pretty purple shoes clicked louder and louder. In the sky, she could see the sun peeking out from behind a cloud and she smiled.

Just then, Della heard a tap behind her. She turned and gasped. People were following her through the village. They were dancing, too! Little children danced with their parents, teenagers did the latest dance moves and there was even an old man, waving his walking stick in the air like a baton.

Dancing Della

Nobody in the village had ever seen anything like it.
By the time Della reached the high street, there was a
crowd of people behind her. Children, mothers, fathers and
grandparents were dancing through the town. The shoppers
hurried to watch, staring in amazement. Cars stopped as drivers
couldn't believe their eyes and shopkeepers came to their doors,
but soon they couldn't help joining in, too.

Della kept dancing, leading the villagers to the Village Green. She twirled and skipped and everyone followed her, forming a huge circle, holding hands and dancing. Della saw Lisa in the crowd and she rushed over and grabbed Lisa's hand, dragging her into the dancing circle. Suddenly, the sun burst through the clouds and shone down on the green, making everyone smile and dance faster.

Dancing Della

As the sun shone brightly, Lisa looked at Della and did
one of their secret dance moves, winking and laughing.
Della tapped out a perfect rhythm, smiling as she thought about
how her shoes had helped her to cheer up the whole village.
Suddenly, Lisa started to clap and the villagers cheered.
"Dancing Della has saved the day!" they cried, smiling at Della
and dancing across the Village Green in the sunshine.

The Purrfect Playmate

Grace had just moved into a new house and she was feeling bored. Her parents were too busy unpacking to play with her and she was feeling fed up. She'd tried doing a jigsaw and reading a book, but what she really wanted was a friend to play with.

Suddenly, Grace heard a miaow. She looked around and saw a beautiful black and white cat running towards her. Grace stroked his beautiful soft fur as he purred contentedly. She looked at the cat's name tag on his collar and smiled. He was called Lucky.

Grace found some wool and ran around with it, wriggling it for Lucky to try to catch. He jumped up, trying to catch the string of wool. Grace held it still and while he lay on his back and played. "Would you like some milk, Lucky?" asked Grace, turning to go inside.

The Purrfect Playmate

When Grace came back outside again she was just in time to see Lucky running across the garden, "Lucky, wait!" she cried, darting after him. Just as she was about to catch up, Lucky jumped over the fence at the end of the garden.

"Come back!" shouted Grace. She climbed up the fence, but brambles caught in her ponytail. "Ouch!" she cried, jumping into next door's garden.

The Purrfect Playmate

Grace looked around, but she couldn't see Lucky anywhere. Suddenly, she saw a flash of black dart across the lawn. Grace raced after Lucky, tripping over a bucket of water and landing in a wet heap on the grass. Quickly, she stood up and was just in time to see Lucky disappear into another garden. Grace darted after him, trying to keep up with the mischievous cat, but where was he going?

Suddenly, Grace saw Lucky up a tree. "There you are!" she cried as Lucky gazed down at her. "You had better come down from there," said Grace. "You might fall." Grace climbed to the lowest branch. She stretched up and up, but she couldn't reach the purring cat. How on earth was she going to rescue him now?

Just then, someone shouted out, "Hey, what are you doing?"

The Purrfect Playmate

Grace looked down to see a boy about her age. "I'm trying to rescue Lucky," said Grace as the boy began to laugh at her. "I'm Adam," he said. "Lucky is my cat and he isn't stuck, he loves to climb trees."

"I'm Grace," said Grace, as she wobbled on the tree branch. Adam quickly fetched a chair and helped Grace down.

"Thank you," said Grace, feeling very silly. She was covered in mud, her clothes were messy and she was dripping wet.

Just at that moment, Lucky jumped down from the tree and rubbed against Grace's legs, purring. Grace smiled at him, as Adam's mother walked over to them. "Hello!" she said, smiling. "You must be Grace from next door. Your parents have invited Adam and I to yours for tea. Shall we go together?" Grace showed Adam and his mother to her house and Lucky followed along behind them. Grace smiled at him.

The Purrfect Playmate

After dinner, Grace and Adam played with Lucky on the carpet.
Adam showed Grace how Lucky liked to chase after his toys and
Grace told Adam how he had played with the ball of wool.

"We can share Lucky," said Adam, smiling at Grace. "He's a
very friendly cat."

"Now I have two new friends," Grace said.

"It's very lucky that I met Lucky," she said, giggling.

The King's Birthday Cake

Princess Polly loved to bake. Whether it was making crunchy cookies, or delicious pies, she adored helping Cook in the kitchen. But, best of all, she loved baking delicious cakes. The only problem was that the queen thought that princesses should always look royal and they should never, ever help in the kitchen. So, Polly kept her baking a secret from her mother.

Today, Cook and Polly were making a yummy cream cake with lots of icing. As Polly dashed about the kitchen, weighing ingredients and pouring mixtures, she couldn't wait to taste the delicious cake.

"Don't get too messy!" Cook warned her. Princess Polly laughed. Even if she didn't get messy, Polly still couldn't imagine her mother allowing her to help in the kitchen.

Just then, as Polly picked up a bag of icing sugar, the queen walked into the kitchen. Polly got such a fright that she jumped causing the icing sugar to puff everywhere and cover Polly's dress and hair.

"What are you doing?" demanded the queen, glaring at Polly.

Polly gulped. "I was just learning to cook," she explained.

"Well, princesses don't cook," said the queen, looking cross.

"You cannot help Cook ever again."

Polly was a good princess. She listened to her mother and didn't help Cook ever again, even though she really wanted to.

One day, Polly heard a terrible shriek from the hall. It was her mother. As Polly dashed into the hall, she wondered what was wrong with the queen.

"Cook is ill!" cried the queen. "There is no-one to bake a cake for your father's birthday party," she shrieked.

In desperation, the queen sent soldiers far and wide to find someone who could make a birthday cake fit for a king.

"It has to be at least a meter tall," the soldiers told everyone. "It must be the most beautiful cake anyone has ever seen. The queen has decreed it."

Soon, the soldiers had asked the entire kingdom, but everyone was scared of the queen. It was said she got so cross that steam came out of her ears!

The King's Birthday Cake

As soon as the soldiers returned with the bad news, Polly grabbed the king and queen and dragged them into the kitchen. "It is time for me to help," Polly announced, looking at the queen to see if she agreed. The queen nodded slowly and Polly immediately started to work. She whisked and stirred, mixed and baked and soon her wonderful cake was in the oven. As her parents watched, they smiled at their talented daughter.

When the cake had cooled, Polly decorated it with blue stars, funky pink flowers and little red hearts. It had lots of different colored icing and Polly had made it out of three cakes.
Each one was filled with delicious cream and there was even a crown, made out of icing, sitting at the very top. The guests said it was the most amazing cake that they had ever seen and the king was thrilled with it.

The King's Birthday Cake

Polly felt proud as she looked at the cake. It sat on a table in the middle of the room, in pride of place for everyone to see. No-one could believe it had been made by Princess Polly. No-one except for Cook. She was feeling a little better and had come to see the marvellous cake. As Polly smiled, Cook winked at her. It seemed that falling ill had been a good plan. Now, Polly would be able to bake whenever she liked!

Tilly's Magic Tiara

It was nearly time for Tilly's dance class. She was excited as her teacher, Miss Bailey, had promised there would be an important announcement.

"Girls!" said Miss Bailey. "I am delighted to tell you that this year, for the first time ever, we are going to put on a ballet show at the Lord Mayor's party."

The girls gasped and looked around at each other. Only the very best dancers were invited to the Lord Mayor's party and the girls were excited to try ballet. Tilly spun around in excitement and tripped, knocking all the girls to the floor. Tilly groaned as her friends tried not to be cross. Tilly had no sense of balance and she was always falling over.

"I'm never going to be able to learn how to pirouette in time," said Tilly, storming into the changing room to practice by herself.

Tilly's Magic Tiara

In the changing room, Tilly was determined not to be clumsy as she tried another pirouette. This time Tilly spun faster and faster, going around and around. Suddenly, she slipped. CRASH! Tilly fell into one of the clothing rails and landed in a heap on the floor, covering herself in clothing. She groaned as she picked herself up off the floor. "I'll just have to try harder," Tilly thought.

Tilly's Magic Tiara

Tilly practiced her dancing every day. She even practiced in the supermarket with her mother. The music was perfect to dance to and the floor was lovely and shiny. As Tilly pirouetted through the isles, she went sliding across the floor.

"Ahh!" she cried as she slid into a tower of cans, sending them flying and startling her mother. I'm just useless," said Tilly, sitting on the floor amongst the cans.

When Tilly got home, she stomped all the way to her bedroom. She'd fallen over so many times, she was aching and didn't want to dance anymore. Tilly tried not to cry as her mother walked into her bedroom. "I've told Miss Bailey I'm not dancing at the Lord Mayor's party," Tilly told her mother.

"Well, I have a surprise for you," said Tilly's mother, handing her a sparkly, silver tiara. "This was your granny's when she was a ballet dancer. Maybe it will bring you luck?"

Tilly shrugged as her mother walked out of the room, but soon she felt better and tried the tiara on. Suddenly, Tilly felt magical and tingly. She got up and tried a pirouette and didn't fall over. "Hooray!" she cried, rushing downstairs to show her mother. Tilly's mother couldn't believe her eyes. Tilly was twirling and pirouetting around the living room.
She looked like a perfect ballerina.

"I suppose you have some little rabbits?" asked Mr Flack, grinning horribly at Annabel and reaching into the box. At first he smiled, then he suddenly realized he was holding a snake. "Aaargh!" he screamed, jumping and dropping Sammy.

Before Annabel could catch him, Sammy landed on the floor and shot away across the hall. He slithered under a chair and out of sight.

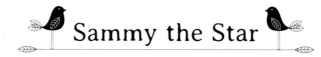

"Catch him, quick, he's poisonous!" cried Mr Flack, putting his hands in the air and running around the hall. There was a terrible noise as everyone jumped up and tried to run away. Budgies squawked, dogs barked and cats meowed as they ran across the room with their owners desperately trying to catch them. In the middle of the chaos, Annabel threw herself at Sammy, grabbing him just before he wriggled away again.

Summer and Starlight

Starlight, the donkey, was the newest arrival at Merrydown Donkey Sanctuary and he wasn't very happy. He pawed at the straw and refused to come out of the trailer. Mrs Rose, the sanctuary owner, had never had such a stubborn guest.

Just then, Summer walked through the gate. "Can I help?" she asked Mrs Rose, running towards the trailer. Summer walked up the ramp and began talking to the nervous donkey, gently stroking his nose. "Come on now, Starlight," she whispered.

To Mrs Rose's surprise, Starlight took a small step forward, then another. Soon, he was out of the trailer. "I think you've made a new friend," said Mrs Rose, smiling.

Summer spent all day playing with Starlight, but soon it was time to go home. "Don't worry, Starlight," she said, quietly. "I'll be back to see you tomorrow."

Summer and Starlight

Early the next day, Summer rushed to see Starlight, but when she got to the sanctuary he was nowhere to be found.

"Oh, no," said Summer, as she and Mrs Rose stared at the field where Starlight had been. Suddenly, Summer noticed a frayed piece of rope. Starlight must have chewed through it, pushed open the gate and escaped out into the village. Summer ran to her bike. She had to find Starlight!

As Summer cycled down the road, she saw Mrs Rice standing in her garden. She looked very cross.

"Whoever's done this is in big trouble!" she cried, pointing to her flower border. Someone had trodden all over Mrs Rice's garden, leaving a trail of flowers leading along the road. Summer thought she could see hoofprints amongst the mess. She began to cycle faster, determined to find Starlight before he caused anymore trouble.

Following the trail of flowers, Summer cycled into the town. Suddenly, she heard a loud shout. "My washing!" cried Mrs Tumble. "I will be very angry when I find out who caused all this mess."

Summer looked at Mrs Tumble's garden, she could see more hoofprints leading around the washing. Summer knew exactly who had made the mess.

Just then, Summer saw a hoof disappearing at the end of Mrs Tumble's garden. It must be Starlight! She quickly ran around the scattered washing, dashing after Starlight. "Wait," called Summer, as she scrambled through a hedge, but she just couldn't catch up with Starlight. Soon, she was covered in mud and had twigs poking out of her hair. No matter how fast she crawled, she would never catch him.

Summer decided to go home and tell her mother about Starlight. As she arrived in her garden, Summer heard a noise. She looked behind her to see Starlight chewing on a flower with a pink, spotty sock hanging from his ear. He made a soft, neighing sound, recognizing Summer. He must have followed her!

Just then, Mrs Tumble, Mrs Rice and Mrs Rose arrived in Summer's garden. "There's the culprit!" they cried together, pointing at Starlight.

Summer and Starlight

"Did Starlight make all of this mess?" asked Summer's mother.
Summer nodded and threw her arms around Starlight's neck.
"It's not his fault," she cried. "He's just a donkey with no home.
I will clean up all of the mess. I promise!"
"Don't worry, Summer," said Mrs Rose, smiling at Summer
and Starlight. "We will clean up the mess together."
"Hee-Haw," said Starlight, loudly and everyone began to laugh.
Starlight was such a funny donkey, Summer thought, smiling.

Message in a Bottle

Kelly had just moved into a new home beside a lagoon and she couldn't wait to explore. She stood up and stretched, "I'm just going for a walk by the lagoon," she told her mother, as she walked along the sand, splashing in the water.

Kelly hadn't gone far when she found a bottle washed up on the beach. She picked it up and was surprised to see a piece of paper rolled up inside. She unrolled it, reading the words, "Please help me! I'm stuck on Dragon Rock!"

Kelly looked across the water. Suddenly, she noticed a rock in the distance, at the end of a sandbank. It looked a little bit like a dragon. There were swirly rocks for eyes and bumps for nostrils. There were even spiky shells for teeth. Kelly quickly ran towards the rock.

To her amazement, Kelly found a girl behind the rock.
She was tangled up in lots of seaweed and looked upset.
Suddenly, Kelly noticed that she had a pink tail, like a dolphin.
The girl was a mermaid!

Kelly quickly started tugging and pulling at the seaweed net
and soon the mermaid was free. "Finally," said Kelly.
"My name's Kelly," she said to the mermaid. "Great to meet you."

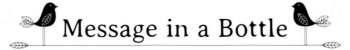

"I'm Coral," said the mermaid, sitting down next to Kelly. "Thank you for helping me. I feel much better now."

Kelly smiled as Coral started to tell her all about being a mermaid. Coral lived in a magic shell castle and she had a dolphin as a best friend. Kelly imagined life under the sea, all of the friendly sea creatures, the huge shell castles and the magic pearls. Coral was so lucky.

As they collected shells from the rock pools and played with one another's hair, Kelly told Coral all about moving house and how she hadn't met any new friends yet. Coral fixed Kelly's hair in place with beautiful, shimmery slides made from seashells all different colors and shades. As Kelly brushed Coral's hair, she thought she was so lucky to have met such a special friend.

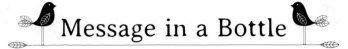

Suddenly, Kelly had an idea. She began to sing a song, dancing along the beach.

"What are you doing?" Coral asked her, watching Kelly and looking confused.

"I'm dancing," said Kelly. "Look." She wiggled and jumped up and down the beach, practicing her dance moves and teaching Coral. Soon, they had made up their very own routine. They wiggled and danced along the beach, giggling together.

The friends had so much fun that Kelly couldn't believe it when her mother called along the beach that it was time for dinner.

Suddenly, Kelly felt sad. Coral was the first friend she had met in her new home and now she had to leave. "Can we hang out together again?" she asked Coral.
"Of course we can," replied Coral, smiling at Kelly.

Kelly couldn't wait until the next time she could see Coral.
They could make pretty jewelry from the shells they had found
and maybe Kelly would ride a dolphin? She smiled, thinking
of how lucky she was that her family had moved here. If they
hadn't, Kelly would have never read the message in the bottle
and she wouldn't have a beautiful mermaid as a friend.

107

Suzy's Special Stone

It was the night before Suzy was due to start her new school. Moving to a new town had been bad enough, but starting a new school was worse. She would be meeting new teachers, having to find her way around. Most scary of all, she had to make new friends. The thought of that made Suzy feel really upset. She was so shy, it took her ages to make friends. Just as she was about to cry, her brother, Simon, walked into the room.

"Don't worry, Suzy" he said, handing her a beautiful stone. "This my magic stone. It always helps me out when I am feeling nervous."

Suzy stared at the stone. It was smooth and shaped like a heart. As she held it tightly, she felt her nerves slip away. Maybe tomorrow would be fun after all?

The next morning, Suzy felt really scared. She stood at the school gate watching the other children go inside. They played, joked and chatted together happily. Suzy reached into her pocket for the stone. As soon as she touched it, she felt happier.

Just then, as if from nowhere, a teacher appeared. "Hello, Suzy," said the teacher. "Would you like to see your new school?" she asked, smiling and beckoning Suzy to follow.

Suzy's Special Stone

When Suzy got to the classroom door, she peered anxiously around it. There were so many people and she didn't know where to sit. She clasped her magic stone again and a friendly girl turned to her.

"Hello, I'm Clare," she said. "Would you like to sit next to me?"

"Yes, please," said Suzy, smiling at Clare and sitting down next to her, keeping the magic stone on the desk, just in case.

At lunch-time, Suzy felt nervous again. She put her hand in her pocket and felt the stone. Just then, Clare looked up at her. "Would you like to sit with us?" she asked, introducing Suzy to her friends, Rosie, Charlie and Megan.

Clare told Suzy all about how they were supposed to be going to Lisa's after school, but Lisa was ill so they couldn't. Suddenly, Suzy had an idea. "Come to my house!" she cried.

After school, Suzy rushed to meet her mother at the school gate. She had the magic stone in her hand. "Mother," she called. "I've had an amazing day at school. I've met lots of new friends and they were supposed to be going to Lisa's tonight, but now they can't because she's ill. Can they come to ours instead?" Suzy's mother laughed. "Of course they can," she said, smiling. "As long as we ask their parent's first."

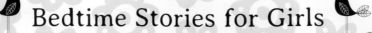

Suzy, Clare, Megan, Charlie and Rosie had a lovely afternoon together, but soon it was time for everyone to go home.
Suzy was sad as she waved goodbye, but then she remembered that she would see them at school tomorrow.

As soon as dinner was ready, Suzy rushed to the table.
She couldn't wait to tell Simon all about her day. She wanted to thank him for giving her the magic stone.

Suzy's Special Stone

Simon smiled and whispered in Suzy's ear. "I'll let you into a secret," he said. "The stone isn't actually magic. Everything that happened today, you did all by yourself. I'm really proud of you."

Suzy looked at Simon and laughed. "I don't mind that it is not a magic stone," she said. "I've had a brilliant day and made lots of new friends. As far as I am concerned, it will always be a special stone to me!"

What's Wrong, Waggy-Tail?

One day, Sally was sitting in the garden when she heard a strange scratching sound. It seemed to be coming from the shed. She tip-toed closer and slowly opened the door. Suddenly, a little dog with floppy ears, brown spots and a very wet nose, came flying out.

"Oh, aren't you gorgeous?!" Sally cried as she knelt down. He leapt up at her, his little tail wagging so fast she thought he'd take off. Sally looked on the little dog's collar, but there was no name-tag. "I'll call you Waggy-Tail," she laughed, cuddling the dog.

Just then, Sally's mother called her to come inside. As she turned around to answer, Waggy-Tail disappeared along the path and out of the garden. Sally sighed, she had always wanted her own dog to look after.

What's Wrong, Waggy-Tail?

That night, Sally couldn't sleep. She kept wondering what had happened to Waggy-Tail. Every time Sally heard a noise she jumped out of bed and looked out of the window.
Suddenly, she saw a movement. Waggy-Tail sat in the garden, looking up at Sally.

Sally rushed into the garden and led Waggy-Tail to the shed, opening the door. "Welcome back, Waggy-Tail," she said. "I'll leave this door open. Then you have somewhere to sleep."

Every day for the next two weeks Waggy-Tail visited Sally. They played games in the shed, hiding from Sally's mother and Sally took Waggy-Tail for walks in the village. She wound her scarf around his collar so she had a lead and walked him proudly, feeling like a proper dog owner. On the way home, Sally went to the pet shop and bought Waggy-Tail real dog food and some bone-shaped doggy treats.

The next day, something seemed very wrong with Waggy-Tail. He didn't want his dog food, or even any of his tasty treats. When he tried to settle down in his bed, he whined and couldn't seem to get comfortable. As Waggy-Tail scratched at his blankets and wriggled, Sally felt worried. She stroked him gently, suddenly noticing that his tummy was swollen. "Oh no," Sally whispered. What if Waggy-Tail was ill?

"Mother!" cried Sally, running into the house.
"Where are you?" On the landing, she noticed that the ladder to the loft had been pulled down. Her mother poked her head through the hatch. "What on earth's the matter, Sally?" she asked, looking confused.

"It's Waggy-Tail!" cried Sally. "I've been looking after him for two weeks. I think I might have poisoned him. He looks so ill." Sally took her mother's hand and pulled her out of the door.

"Who's Waggy-Tail?" Sally's mum asked, opening the shed door.
As they looked inside, Sally and her mother gasped.
Waggy-Tail was surrounded by five tiny puppies. He was a she!
"Oh, Waggy-Tail, aren't you clever?" Sally said. "So that's why
you were so hungry and fat," she said, giggling.
"This looks like Maisie, Mrs Mason's dog" said Sally's mother.
Waggy-Tail's ears pricked up at the mention of her name.

Sally's face fell. She didn't know Waggy-Tail had an owner. "Don't look so sad," said her mother. "You've taken such good care of Maisie, I'll ask Mrs. Mason if you can have one of her puppies to look after."

Sally was so happy. It didn't matter that Waggy-Tail belonged to someone else. They would always be friends and now and Sally would have her own puppy to look after. Sally was going to be very busy from now on!

Megan's Magic Bracelet

Megan was fed up of her little brother annoying her. She stormed into the garden. "At least I will get some peace out here," Megan said, sighing. Megan sat next to her flower border and started to dig away at the weeds. Instead of Sam's annoying shouts, she could hear beautiful bird song and the flowers she'd planted looked so pretty.

As she dug, Megan imagined she was a treasure-seeker, searching for buried treasure. CLINK! Suddenly her trowel hit something hard in the ground. Was it another stone?

Megan dug a little more. There, under the soil, was a dirty metal chain. She hurriedly rubbed at it with a hanky from her pocket. As she cleared away the dirt, Megan could see that it was silver underneath. She really had found treasure! As Megan held it up, she could see that it was a beautiful silver bracelet, sparkling in the sunshine.

Megan's Magic Bracelet

As Megan looked closely at the bracelet, she could just make out some words on it. They said, Three Wishes For You. Just then, Sam came charging at her from across the garden. He trampled all over her flowers and tried to grab the bracelet from her. "Pirate treasure!" he cried.

"You are annoying, Sam," said Megan, turning away. "I wish you would turn into a nice, quiet frog." When she looked back, Sam was gone.

Suddenly, Sam disappeared. In his place was a green frog that hopped around Megan's feet. Megan stared at the slimy green creature. "Is that you, Sam?" she asked.

The frog hopped up and down even more. "Yes, it's me!" the frog cried in Sam's voice. "Wow! I've always wondered what it's like to be a frog. It's brilliant!"

"Come back!" cried Megan as Sam hopped around the garden. Before she could catch Sam, he hopped into the pond. SPLASH! He swam in and out of the lily pads, startling the little goldfish and tadpoles.

"Sam," hissed Megan. "You come out of the pond right now." Just then, Megan heard her mother calling. "Dinner will be ready in five minutes." Megan had just five minutes to get Sam to come out of the pond and stop being a frog!

Suddenly, something very wet, green and squelchy flew out
of the pond and landed in Megan's lap. "Ugh!" she cried,
just managing to catch Sam. "Stop being a frog." she said,
desperately holding onto him.

"Catch me if you can!" cried Sam, wriggling out of her hands.

"Oh, I wish you'd go back to being a boy again," said Megan, as
Sam hopped towards the kitchen.

Just then, there was a flash and Sam, the boy, was sitting next to Megan. "This magic bracelet gave me three wishes," said Megan, showing it to Sam.

"That means that there's one wish left," said Sam. "I could be a pirate or a fish or an elephant..."

"You could," said Megan, "but then you'd miss having sausage and chips for tea."

Suddenly, Megan had an idea. "I wish that we could have an extra special treat for after tea." There was another flash and cupcakes appeared around Sam, landing in his lap.

"Yum," said Sam, smiling at Megan and picking up the cupcakes to take to the kitchen. "Let's bury the bracelet again," he said. "Then someone else can have a special treat, like us."

Megan smiled at Sam. She'd had enough magic for one day, too.

The Mermaidettes

Jessica was really enjoying her day with her mermaid friends, Crystal and Chelsea. They were having a lovely picnic on a sand island far out in the blue ocean. After a while, they got a bit bored. "What shall we do next?" asked Chelsea.

"Let's sing a song!" replied Jessica and she began to sing a lovely tune. Soon, Chelsea and Crystal joined in. "We should start our own band," said the mermaids, laughing.

"That's a great idea!" cried Jessica. "All we need is some instruments." She thought for a moment. "I know," she said, "Let's use shells and make cool sounds that way." Jessica jumped into the water with a splash and disappeared beneath the waves. Chelsea and Crystal dived after her, feeling excited as they followed their friend.

The Mermaidettes

The mermaids dived down into the sea, laughing about which instruments they wanted to play in their band. When they reached the bottom of the sea, they started looking for shells. "Look at this!" cried Jessica, holding up a swirly shell and singing into it. Her voice sounded perfect as it echoed all around the reef.

Soon, the girls had all found shells and they swam back to the sandy island. They were excited to start practicing.

"Wow," cried Chelsea, pulling on a piece of seaweed. A loud, twanging sound echoed over the reef. Then, Chelsea tied the seaweed to either end of her shell, adding a few more strings. As she pulled on them, they made lots of different noises.

Just then, Crystal began to tap on the top of one of her shells. It made a loud booming sound, beating out a tune as Chelsea pulled on the seaweed strings. The girls began to giggle as the music floated over the water.

Suddenly, Jessica remembered about Sandy Cove. Sandy Cove was a big cave in the middle of the ocean. The girls could go there to practice properly.

"Come on!" she cried to her friends, jumping into the sea and swimming towards the cave. Jessica couldn't wait to start singing. Just then, she remembered that their band didn't have a name. "Hmm," wondered Jessica, thinking about what they could be called as she swam across the waves.

The girls were ready to play as soon as they got to Sandy Cove. "1...2...3...4...," Crystal cried, tapping the booming shell. Jessica leaned towards her shell and began to sing and Chelsea began to play on her seaweed instrument. As the girls finished their first song, a crowd had gathered and they began to cheer. "Thank you," called Jessica to the dancing crowd. "We are The Mermaidettes," she said, smiling and waving. The Mermaidettes was the best idea that Jessica had ever had!

Beautiful Ballerinas

Katie and her friends were practicing for a surprise ballet show. The girls' dance teacher, Miss Satin, was retiring and they wanted to give her a lovely surprise. Unfortunately, it was going very wrong. In fact, it was a mess. No matter how many times they tried to work out a routine, they just couldn't get the steps right without Miss Satin. Megan played a tune on the piano, but it didn't seem to help the girls, as they wobbled around the room.

Just then, there was a strange banging on the other side of the door and Katie came into the room. She was pulling a big chest. "Look what I've found," Katie said to her friends, puffing as she dragged the heavy chest across the floor. "I found it in the costume cupboard. You never know, there might just be something in here to inspire us."

The girls rushed over as Katie opened the chest. They gasped as she pulled out a sparkly fairy dress. "Look!" cried Katie, as she pulled out more and more dresses. There were enough for all the girls and there were even some fairy wings and wands with pretty stars on the end.

"We can be fairies in our show for Miss Satin!" cried Katie, holding up the sparkly, pink dress and dancing around with her friends, laughing and smiling.

Beautiful Ballerinas

The dresses were perfect. The skirts were covered with sequins and they sparkled brightly as the girls tried them on, laughing and giggling with each other. Each girl found a fairy dress to fit her and everyone looked so pretty.

The girls danced around the room, twirling and pirouetting in their outfits. Suddenly, Katie noticed something, half-hidden, at the bottom of the chest. Looking more closely, she saw that it was a music box.

Katie lifted the delicate, pink lid and a tinkling song began to play. Four ballerinas danced and swayed in time to the music. As the girls watched, they wished they could dance as well as the ballerinas in the box. They looked so elegant and graceful. Suddenly, Katie had an idea. "Why don't we learn this dance?" she said. "It would be perfect for Miss Satin's surprise show."

Beautiful Ballerinas

The girls thought Katie's idea was brilliant. They jumped up and tried to follow the movement of the music box ballerinas. It was great fun, but hard work. At first they were a bit clumsy, but soon they twirled and spun as delicate and graceful as real ballerinas. Katie couldn't wait to dance for Miss Satin. "Don't forget to invite your parents to our show," Katie called, as they left to go home. "Remember to tell them it's a secret."

On the night of the show, the girls hid backstage. As the spotlights turned on, Katie suddenly felt nervous.

Just then, the tinkling music of the music box began to play and she danced onto the stage with her friends.

Katie pirouetted perfectly across the stage, spotting Miss Satin in the crowd. She had a huge smile on her face and her eyes glittered with sparkly tears.

As the applause died down, Katie called Miss Satin onto
the stage. She handed her a beautiful bouquet of flowers.
"Thank you so much," said Miss Satin. "I have a little surprise
for you, too," she said, handing each girl a music box with a
tiny ballerina inside. "You are all such beautiful ballerinas,"
said Miss Satin. "Now you will have something to help you
remember me."

Lisa's Surprising Spells

It was nearly time for the annual spelling exams and everyone in Fairy Land was busy practicing their magic. Everyone apart from Lisa. All day, Lisa's magic had been going wrong. "I'm the fairy who can't do magic," she said to her sister, Mia. "I'm going to fail my exam tomorrow."

"You won't fail," said Mia. "I'll help you practice."

Lisa smiled and picked up her wand. "Okay," she said. "I'm going to magic your hair pink." She waved her wand and suddenly there was a flash. Lisa looked at Mia, her hair was pink all right. It was sweet and fluffy, too. For a moment, Lisa thought the spell had worked, then she looked closer. She had turned Mia's hair into candy floss!

"Oh, I'm so sorry!" cried Lisa, trying not to giggle, but Mia did not look happy. "Just don't eat it," Mia grumbled as she walked away, waving her wand and turning her hair back to normal.

Lisa's Surprising Spells

The next morning, Lisa got to school early so she could practice for her exam. As usual, everything was going wrong. She groaned when instead of lifting the book shelf, all of the books turned into birds and when she tried to magic it back, she somehow managed to turn the classroom desks into frogs. Lisa stood in the middle of the room, surrounded by feathers and frogs and sighed. She would never pass her exam.

Just then, her teacher, Miss Silverwing, arrived.

"Why don't you practice with me?" Miss Silverwing suggested.

Lisa's Surprising Spells

Lisa practiced all morning with Miss Silverwing, but it didn't seem to help. Birds turned into frogs and frogs turned into tiaras. At one point, Miss Silverwing's earrings turned into ice-cream cones. "Mmmm! Delicious," said Miss Silverwing, eating the cone of one of her earrings. "Don't worry, Lisa," she said, smiling. "Just try again."

Lisa looked at the frog filled classroom and waved her wand. Suddenly, all the books were back on the shelves and the frogs began to turn back into desks.

Soon, it was time for Lisa's exam and despite Miss Silverwing's help, she felt nervous. First, Lisa had to magic some hair-slides. She wished for butterfly slides and they fluttered gently onto her head. Finally, for the last test, she had to conjure a bouquet of flowers. Lisa whispered her spell quietly and suddenly, there was a flash as lots of pretty daisies fluttered from the end of her wand, covering her and the fairy who was taking the exam. Lisa sighed, at least the exam was finished.

"Lisa," cried Miss Silverwing as Lisa left the exam hall. "You've passed!" Lisa was speechless as Miss Silverwing handed her the special spelling exam certificate. Even though Lisa hadn't performed the spells perfectly, she could still do magic. She was a proper fairy!

Just then, Mia arrived at the school. "I knew you could do it," she said. "You're very clever," she whispered to Lisa, giving her a big cuddle. "Your magic will only get better now."

Princess Posy and the Undoing Potion

Princess Posy sat beside the palace fountain and sighed. Her best friend, Princess Jessica, had moved away last year and Posy missed her. The strange thing was that no-one knew where Jessica had gone. Just then, a little brown rabbit hopped up to Posy.

"I'm Jessica," the rabbit said, as Posy stared in amazement. The witch of the forest cast a spell on me and I can only be changed back if someone gets the Undoing Potion from her."

"I'll help you, Jessica," said Posy. "I'll ride through the dark forest to the wicked witch's tower and get the potion."

Posy dashed off to get her pony, Casper. The dark forest was a dangerous place. It was made up of knights who had been turned into trees by the wicked witch. Posy would need the help of Casper if she was going to sneak into her tower.

Princess Posy and The Undoing Potion

Even though the forest was dark and the trees looked like they were reaching out to grab her, Posy wasn't scared. She knew that if the knights could move, they would help her rescue Princess Jessica from the evil witch.

In the distance, Posy could just see the witch's tower. Smoke was rising from the top and Posy could see her in the window. She patted Casper and he tossed his head and neighed bravely. He wasn't scared either.

Princess Posy and The Undoing Potion

When they reached the bottom of the tower, Posy hid Casper carefully and ran to a small hole in the wall. Posy squeezed through the gap, reaching the bottom of a winding staircase leading towards the witch's Potion Room. As Posy crept silently up the stairs, she could see lots of strange plants with creepy eyes, books with teeth and jars of worms. There were huge spiders, potion bottles and a giant bat fluttered in the air.

At the top of the stairs, Posy's heart began to thump.
The witch was so interested in her evil potion, that she didn't
notice Posy push open the door and creep into the room.
The Undoing Potion was on a shelf beside the witch. If only
Posy could stretch a little further, she would reach it.
Just then, the witch turned around, shrieking as she saw Posy.
She waved her wand and Posy ducked under the spell, grabbing
the potion and landing on the floor.

The witch's spell just missed Posy, hitting the bookshelves and scattering weird plants, books, spiders and worms across the Potion Room. Posy tried to ignore them as she rolled out of the witch's way, gripping the Undoing Potion tightly.

Suddenly, the witch was standing above Posy and raising her wand. Posy took a deep breath and leapt at the witch, knocking her over and dashing out of the room, down the winding staircase and out of the door.

Posy leapt on Casper's back and they galloped away. The witch was behind her, casting spells in every direction and sending lightning bolts across the forest. As Posy and Casper dashed in and out of the trees, just missing the witch's spells, the Undoing Potion slipped from Posy's pocket and began to drip onto the forest floor. Suddenly, there was a flash and a shiny knight appeared beside Posy.

Princess Posy and The Undoing Potion

All around Posy, there were flashes as trees turned magically into knights. They marched on the witch, forcing her back to her tower and deflecting her spells with their shields.

Suddenly, Posy noticed there were only a few drops of the Undoing Potion left. She had to get back to Jessica. As the knights fought the witch, Posy and Casper galloped across the forest, racing to the palace.

Posy rushed into the gardens, giving Jessica the last drops of the Undoing Potion. Suddenly, there was a flash and Jessica appeared, surrounded by little clouds and sparkles. Posy smiled giving her friend a cuddle. For the rest of the day, she and Jessica walked in the gardens, telling one another about their adventures with the witch.

After that, the witch was never heard of ever again.
Princess Posy grew up to be a famous queen and she was known across the land for her army of mysterious shiny knights.